by Nat Gabriel
illustrated by Terry Taylor

Scott Foresman

Editorial Offices: Glenview, Illinois • New York, New York
Sales Offices: Reading, Massachusetts • Duluth, Georgia
Glenview, Illinois • Carrollton, Texas • Menlo Park, California

You can not read a word.
You can not say a word.

But you can dance.

Do what I do.

Left. Left.

Step. Step. Step.

Do what I do. Left. Left.

Ow!

Do what I do.

Left. Left.

Ow!

Do what I do.
Left. Left.

Oh, no!

Say it with me.

Left. Left.

Step. Step. Step.

Say it again.

This way. That way.

Step. Step. Step.

Left. Left.

Step. Step. Step.

You are good at it!

Now I will do what you do.
Take a nap!